Jimmy watched his radar monitor. "He does not seem to be chasing the bone anymore. I wonder what distracted him," said Carl.

GODDARD

"It looks like Goddard found a friend," said Jimmy. "That beagle is leading him toward a house."

Sheen slapped Jimmy on the back.

"See, he is having the time of his life. Hey, why don't we go to Retroland?" he asked. "Not now," said Jimmy. "There's something strange about those people."

"Hey! They are putting Goddard in a cage!"
cried Jimmy, leaping to his feet.
"They can't be taking him to a pound,"
said Carl. "Goddard is not a real dog."
The people put the cage in their car and
drove away. The beagle chased after them.

The boys jumped on their bikes and sped across town.

"Hurry!" Jimmy shouted.

"He might end up as scrap metal—or worse!" Carl cried.

"Thanks a lot, Carl!" yelled Jimmy.

They followed the radar signal in
Goddard's collar to a factory.
A sign outside read,
ROBOTICS, INC.
"That couple must work here," said Jimmy.
Carl pulled on the doors, but they would
not budge.

"Ultra Lord, grant me the power to open this window!" Sheen cried.
The window opened easily and Jimmy climbed in after Sheen.
With a little help from his friends, Carl made it through too.

The boys saw an empty cage.
"It looks like Goddard ate the lock," said
Jimmy. "That's my pal!"
"I think I hear someone!" Carl cried.
"Get behind those boxes!" Jimmy
commanded as the strange couple
entered the room.
"The robot dog is gone!" hissed the man.

"We must find him. Our robot army
needs his technology to take over
the world," said the woman.
Suddenly they removed their masks.
"Leaping leptons," Jimmy whispered.
"They are robots! We have to stop
them!"

Suddenly two robots spotted them and started dragging Sheen away! Jimmy rushed at the robots.

He pulled the main control panel off one robot, and then the other. The robots froze in place.

"Come on guys," yelled Jimmy. "Let's finish off the rest of them!"

Jimmy, Carl, and Sheen zoomed around the room, removing the robots' control boxes.

After all the robots were frozen,
they searched the factory.
"What if Goddard is lost forever?"
Jimmy said sadly.
Then from under a pile of boxes
came a beeping noise. The boys dug
like crazy.